The Nursery
"ALICE"

By LEWIS CARROLL

With a New Introduction by
MARTIN GARDNER

The Nursery
"ALICE"

DOVER PUBLICATIONS, INC.

New York

Library of Congress Catalog Card Number: 66-24136

Manufactured in the United States of America
Dover Publications, Inc.
180 Varick Street
New York 14, N. Y.

INTRODUCTION.

"IT IS ONE of the mysteries of publishing that this charming book ... has been out of print for so many years. As a book for children under five, it is only surpassed by the best of Beatrix Potter...." So wrote Roger Lancelyn Green, commenting on *The Nursery Alice,* in *The Diaries of Lewis Carroll,* which he so admirably edited.*

Since Green made those comments, in 1954, there have been rumors of forthcoming reprints of *The Nursery Alice,* by both English and American publishers, but the promised books failed to materialize. But now, as a companion piece to its earlier facsimile of *Alice's Adventures Under Ground,* the publisher has produced this facsimile volume of the second edition of *The Nursery Alice.* It would have been easy to reproduce from the first, but since Carroll thought the colors of that edition too gaudy, it seemed best to use the one he approved.

*The Diaries of Lewis Carroll, Roger Lancelyn-Green, ed. (New York, Oxford University Press, 1954), Vol. II, p. 469.

v

The first mention of *The Nursery Alice* in Carroll's *Diary* is an entry for March 29, 1885. "Never before," he writes, "have I had so many literary projects on hand at once. For curiosity I will here make a list of them." Fifteen projects are cited. The ninth is *The Nursery Alice*, "for which twenty pictures are now being coloured by Mr. Tenniel." On July 10 he records that Tenniel had finished the pictures, but it is not until December 28, 1888, almost four years later, that he writes: "Began text of *The Nursery Alice*." Less than two months later, on February 20, 1889, an entry reads: "Sent off last of MS. for *The Nursery Alice*." On April 18 he writes that he completed checking page proofs.

But Carroll was a difficult man to please with respect to a book's appearance. Charles Morgan, in *The House of Macmillan: 1843–1943* (Macmillan, 1943), says that ten thousand copies of *The Nursery Alice* were printed, but that Carroll took one look at them and decided that the pictures were too gaudy. "No copy, he said,"—I quote from Morgan —"was to be sold in England; all were to be offered to America. They were offered, and declined as not being gaudy enough."

A second edition of ten thousand was scheduled, but now Macmillan made sure that Carroll saw advance copies, completely bound, before the final print run. Carroll rejected the uncolored samples sent to him in September, 1889, because the March Hare on the back cover was off-center. "As to how many copies we can sell I care absolutely nothing," he wrote to his publishers (I quote from Green's *Lewis Carroll*, a Bodley Head monograph published in 1960); "the only thing I *do* care for is, that all copies that *are* sold shall be artistically first-rate." A dozen copies with color, sent to him in October, were also returned, because the covers cracked when he opened them and the leaves had a tendency to curl.

Samples were finally approved by the end of October, and pages for the new edition were printed by late February, 1890. "Received from Mr. E. Evans a finished set of the sheets of *The Nursery Alice*," Carroll wrote in his *Diary* on March 7, 1890. "It is a *great* success. We can now publish at Easter." On March 25, Lewis Carroll speaks of a trip to London to inscribe a hundred copies of what must have been bound volumes.

Exactly what happened to all ten thousand copies of the first edition is not known. There is a record of four thousand having been sent to the United States, and five hundred to Australia. Many were probably given to hospitals in England and elsewhere. Copies of the first edition are said to be identifiable by the brighter colors of the pictures and by an off-white paper in contrast to the purer white of the second edition, but points on the variant states of the two editions are far from established, and the situation is one of great bibliographic confusion.

There is also a mystery about whether Tenniel himself actually colored the pictures. Carroll's *Diary* speaks as if he did, and in a letter written as late as April 1, 1889, he writes of hoping to get the book published by Easter, and that it contains "pictures enlarged and coloured by Tenniel." But when the book was advertised as "in preparation" in Macmillan's 1886 facsimile of *Alice's Adventures Under Ground*, its pictures are said to be "enlarged and coloured under the Artist's superintendence." In the Macmillan edition of this book, a similar advertisement, as well as its title page, speak of "coloured enlargements from Tenniel's illustrations." What probably happened was that Carroll originally hoped that Tenniel would do the job himself, but that Tenniel finally delegated the work to someone else. (Later, in 1911, *Alice's Adventures in Wonderland* and *Through the Looking-Glass* were brought out by Macmillan in one volume, with sixteen pictures that *were* colored by Tenniel.)

Carroll liked to dedicate his children's books to child-friends, often concealing their names in acrostic poems. *The Nursery Alice* is dedicated to Marie Van der Gucht, whose full name is read by taking the second letter of each line in the dedicatory poem. Marie was a friend of Climene

Mary Holiday, a niece of Henry Holiday, the man who illustrated *The Hunting of the Snark*. Carroll's *Game of Logic*, included in *Symbolic Logic and the Game of Logic*, had earlier been dedicated to Climene with a similar second-letter acrostic.

Carroll first met Marie on July 24, 1885, when she was eleven. His *Diary* records taking her to see *The Mikado* on April 10, 1886, and traveling again to London on September 1 to escort her to the beach at Eastbourne. "Marie and I," he writes the following day, "after a little Bible-reading and letter-writing, spent the morning on the beach...." On November 15 he obtained Marie's mother's permission for the girl to pose as Sylvie in Harry Furniss's illustrations for *Sylvie and Bruno*, but Furniss later revealed that he never took this suggestion seriously, and used his own daughter as the model. On December 30, 1886, Carroll took Marie and another girl to see the operetta of *Alice in Wonderland*, in London. Marie was sixteen in 1890 when *The Nursery Alice* was published. There are two more entries about her in the *Diary*. On August 24, 1895: "Dear Marie Van der Gucht came on a visit to me." And on August 30: "Marie went home again. Her week with me has been very pleasant, to both of us, I think. The Schusters have twice had her up to their house for lawn-tennis; and she and I have spent several evenings at Devonshire Park."

Why Carroll retold in simpler terms the story of Alice's first dream is plain enough from his sentimental preface, but one suspects that another reason may have been that he wanted a book of his own to give away to very young girls when he met them on trains or at the seaside. An entry in his *Diary* (October 1, 1891) reads: "I made friends with a sweet-looking little girl, Constance Linnell, grand-child of the painter. Of course I afterwards sent her *The Nursery Alice*." The "of course" suggests that many copies of this book were given away to the "dimpled darlings" who were too young to read the other *Alice*. In Carroll's opinion, the age at which a child became too old for *The Nursery Alice* varied with the child's economic background. Florence Becker Lennon, in her *Life of Lewis Carroll,* quotes an amusing passage on this from a letter Carroll wrote to his friend Gertrude Thomson, the artist who illustrated his book of poems, *Three Sunsets,* and who designed and colored the covers of *The Nursery Alice:*

> I have just promised to give the little girl, of the porter who always carries my luggage, a book: and had intended it to be *The Nursery Alice,* as the child is 10, and I consider children of the lower orders to be 2 or 3 years behind the upper orders. But a lady, whom I consulted, advised me to give the real *Alice,* as probably more interesting, even now, to the child (they certainly do get very well taught now-a-days), and certainly of more permanent interest.

How successful is *The Nursery Alice* when read today to an English or American boy or girl, upper or lower, age 0 to 5? I prefer not to guess. In some ways the language seems patronizing, but one must admit that Carroll has retold Alice's dream in a way that is easily understood by small children. The story has been shortened to about one-fourth its original length, the verse (except for the nursery rhyme about the Knave of Hearts) has been left out, and of course everything has been skillfully simplified. The only new episode is one about a puppy named Dash who doesn't like his oatmeal porridge (page 22), a digression so dull that one suspects Carroll must have put it in because it referred to an actual incident involving the pet of one of his child-friends. There is a delightful bit of word play (page 19) about the room being as full of Alice as a jar is full of jam. At two places he suggests something whimsical to do with the book itself: shaking it to make the White Rabbit tremble with fright (page 2), and bending up a lower corner of page 36 to see Alice (on the under leaf) looking up at the Cheshire Cat's grin (on the upper leaf).

This was the first time that color had been used for the *Alice* illus-

trations in book publication, and Carroll took advantage of the oppor-
tunity to add many descriptive color words that he had not used before:
the green eyes of the Cheshire Cat, the Mad Hatter's yellow tie with red
spots, the red flamingo in the croquet game, and so on. His comments on
Tenniel's drawings show how seriously he took the illustrations. The
Blue Caterpillar's nose and chin, Carroll explains (page 27), are really
two legs. On page 53 he carefully identifies all twelve jurors in the picture. He calls attention to the foxglove plant on page 34, growing near
the tree in which the Cheshire Cat is grinning, and explains that the
foxglove was once called "Folk's-Gloves," with reference to the fairies
who were spoken of as the "good folk" or "little folk."*

A note headed "Cautions to Readers," that Carroll added to the
book's advertising pages (following the Easter and Christmas Greetings
in the original edition), is worth a comment. Its second part refers to an
unkind review of *Alice's Adventures in Wonderland* that had been written
by someone named Edward Salmon. Salmon had accused Carroll of bor-
rowing from a book by Tom Hood that actually had been published nine
years after the *Alice* book. Carroll's restrained reply does no more than
correct Salmon's error on the date of Hood's book. (Lengthy quotations
from Salmon's review can be found in Appendix B of Mrs. Lennon's
biography of Carroll.)

The real Alice, Alice Liddell, always remained in Carroll's memory
as his favorite child-friend. She was in her late thirties and happily married when *The Nursery Alice,* the fourth and last of his published *Alice*
books, appeared. Carroll was fifty-eight. His first meeting with Reginald

---

*According to J. Worth Estes and Paul Dudley White (in their article, "William Withering and
the Purple Foxglove," *Scientific American,* June, 1965), an equally respectable theory makes the word
a corruption of "foxes-glew," an old Saxon word for "fox music." This was a type of music produced
by an ancient instrument consisting of bells hanging from an arched support, and which the foxglove
blossoms presumably resemble as much as they resemble gloved fingers. The plant's leaves are a source
of digitalis, a drug long used in treating heart disease.

Gervis Hargreaves (who had married Alice in 1880) occurred on November 1, 1888, two months before he began to write *The Nursery Alice*. "It was not easy," Carroll then wrote in his *Diary*, "to link in one's mind the new face with the olden memory—the stranger with the once-so-intimately known and loved 'Alice,' whom I shall always remember best as an entirely fascinating little seven-year-old maiden."

On December 9, 1891, a year after the appearance of *The Nursery Alice*, the last entry about Alice Liddell appears in Carroll's *Diary*. She had been visiting the Deanery of Christ Church and he had invited her to his rooms for tea. "She could not do this, but very kindly came over, with Rhoda [her sister], for a short time in the afternoon."

One has a feeling that, in the closing line of *The Nursery Alice*, Carroll was speaking directly to Alice Liddell; his words echoing that sad farewell of the White Knight as he rode slowly and precariously off into the chessboard forest behind the looking-glass. "Good-bye, Alice dear, good-bye!"

MARTIN GARDNER

Hastings-on-Hudson, New York
April, 1966

The cover design for the original edition

THE NURSERY "ALICE."

[*See p.* 50.

THE NURSERY "ALICE"

CONTAINING TWENTY COLOURED ENLARGEMENTS

FROM

TENNIEL'S ILLUSTRATIONS

TO

"ALICE'S ADVENTURES IN WONDERLAND"

WITH TEXT ADAPTED TO NURSERY READERS

BY

LEWIS CARROLL

THE COVER DESIGNED AND COLOURED

BY

E. GERTRUDE THOMSON

PRICE ONE SHILLING

London

MACMILLAN AND CO.

1890

LONDON
ENGRAVED AND PRINTED
BY
EDMUND EVANS

A Nursery Darling.

A Mother's breast:
Safe refuge from her childish fears,
From childish troubles, childish tears,
Mists that enshroud her dawning years!
See how in sleep she seems to sing
A voiceless psalm — an offering
Raised, to the glory of her King,
    In Love: for Love is Rest.

A Darling's kiss:
Dearest of all the signs that fleet
From lips that lovingly repeat
Again, again, their message sweet!
Full to the brim with girlish glee,
A child, a very child is she,
Whose dream of Heaven is still to be
    At Home: for Home is Bliss.

PREFACE.

(ADDRESSED TO ANY MOTHER.)

I HAVE reason to believe that "Alice's Adventures in Wonderland" has been read by some hundreds of English Children, aged from Five to Fifteen : also by Children, aged from Fifteen to Twenty-five : yet again by Children, aged from Twenty-five to Thirty-five : and even by Children —— for there *are* such —— Children in whom no waning of health and strength, no weariness of the solemn mockery, and the gaudy glitter, and the hopeless misery, of Life has availed to parch the pure fountain of joy that wells up in all child-like hearts —— Children of a "certain" age, whose tale of years must be left untold, and buried in respectful silence.

And my ambition *now* is (is it a vain one?) to be read by Children aged from Nought to Five. To be read? Nay, not so!

PREFACE *(continued)*.

Say rather to be thumbed, to be cooed over, to be dogs'-eared, to be rumpled, to be kissed, by the illiterate, ungrammatical, dimpled Darlings, that fill your Nursery with merry uproar, and your inmost heart of hearts with a restful gladness!

Such, for instance, as a child I once knew, who —— having been carefully instructed that *one* of any earthly thing was enough for any little girl; and that to ask for *two* buns, *two* oranges, *two* of anything, would certainly bring upon her the awful charge of being "greedy" —— was found one morning sitting up in bed, solemnly regarding her *two* little naked feet, and murmuring to herself, softly and penitently, "deedy!"

Easter-tide, 1890.

CONTENTS.

I.

THE WHITE RABBIT.

ONCE upon a time, there was a little girl called Alice : and she had a very curious dream.

Would you like to hear what it was that she dreamed about?

Well, this was the *first* thing that happened. A White Rabbit came running by, in a great hurry ; and, just as it passed Alice, it stopped, and took its watch out of its pocket.

Wasn't *that* a funny thing? Did *you* ever see a Rabbit that had a watch, and a pocket to put it in? Of course, when a Rabbit has a watch, it *must* have a pocket to put it in : it would never do to carry it about in its mouth ——and it wants its hands sometimes, to run about with.

Hasn't it got pretty pink eyes (I think *all* White Rabbits have pink eyes); and pink ears; and a nice brown coat; and you can just see its red pocket-handkerchief peeping out of its coat-pocket : and, what with its blue neck-tie and its yellow waistcoat, it really is *very* nicely dressed.

"Oh dear, oh dear!" said the Rabbit. "I shall be too late!" *What* would it be too late *for*, I wonder? Well, you see, it had to go and visit the Duchess (you'll see a picture of the Duchess, soon, sitting in her kitchen): and the Duchess was a very cross old lady : and the Rabbit *knew* she'd be very angry indeed if he kept her waiting. So the poor thing was as frightened as frightened could be (Don't you see how he's trembling? Just shake the book a little, from side to side, and you'll soon see him tremble), because he thought the Duchess would have his head cut off, for a punishment. That was what the Queen of Hearts used to do, when *she* was angry with people (you'll see a picture of *her*, soon): at least she used to *order* their heads to be cut off, and she always *thought* it was done, though they never *really* did it.

And so, when the White Rabbit ran away, Alice wanted to see what would happen to it : so she ran after it : and she ran, and she ran, till she tumbled right down the rabbit-hole.

And then she had a very long fall indeed. Down, and down, and down, till she began to wonder if she was going right *through* the World, so as to come out on the other side !

It was just like a very deep well : only there was no water in it. If anybody *really* had such a fall as that, it would kill them, most likely : but you know it doesn't hurt a bit to fall in a *dream*, because, all the time you *think* you're falling, you really *are* lying somewhere, safe and sound, and fast asleep !

However, this terrible fall came to an end at last, and down came Alice on a heap of sticks and dry leaves.   But she wasn't a bit hurt, and up she jumped, and ran after the Rabbit again.

And so that was the beginning of Alice's curious dream.   And, next time you see a White Rabbit, try and fancy *you're* going to have a curious dream, just like dear little Alice.

II.

HOW ALICE GREW TALL.

AND so, after Alice had tumbled down the rabbit-hole, and had run a long long way underground, all of a sudden she found herself in a great hall, with doors all round it.

But all the doors were locked: so, you see, poor Alice couldn't get out of the hall: and that made her very sad.

However, after a little while, she came to a little table, all made of glass, with three legs (There are *two* of the legs in the picture, and just the *beginning* of the other leg, do you see?), and on the table was a little key : and she went round the hall, and tried if she could unlock any of the doors with it.

Poor Alice ! The key wouldn't unlock *any* of the doors. But at last she came upon a tiny little door : and oh, how glad she was, when she found the key would fit it !

So she unlocked the tiny little door, and she stooped down and looked through it, and what do you think she saw? Oh, such a beautiful garden ! And she did so *long* to go into it ! But the door was *far* too small. She couldn't squeeze herself through, any more than *you* could squeeze yourself into a mouse-hole !

So poor little Alice locked up the door, and took the key back to the table again : and *this* time she found quite a new thing on it (now look at the picture again), and what do you think it was? It was a little bottle, with a label tied to it, with the words "DRINK ME" on the label.

So she tasted it : and it was *very* nice : so she set to work, and drank it up. And then *such* a curious thing happened to her! You'll never guess what it was : so I shall have to tell you. She got smaller, and smaller, till at last she was just the size of a little doll!

Then she said to herself " *Now* I'm the right size to get through the little door!" And away she ran. But, when she got there, the door was locked, and the key was on the top of the table, and she couldn't reach it! *Wasn't* it a pity she had locked up the door again?

Well, the next thing she found was a little cake : and it had the words " EAT ME " marked on it. So of course she set to work and ate it up. And *then* what do you think happened to her? No, you'll never guess! I shall have to tell you again.

She grew, and she grew, and she grew. Taller than she was before! Taller than *any* child! Taller than any grown-up person! Taller, and taller, and taller! Just look at the picture, and you'll *see* how tall she got!

Which would *you* have liked the best, do you think, to be a little tiny Alice, no larger than a kitten, or a great tall Alice, with your head always knocking against the ceiling?

III.

THE POOL OF TEARS.

PERHAPS you think Alice must have been very much pleased, when she had eaten the little cake, to find herself growing so tremendously tall? Because of course it would be easy enough, *now*, to reach the little key off the glass table, and to open the little tiny door.

Well, of course she could do *that :* but what good was it to get the door open, when she couldn't get *through?* She was worse off than ever, poor thing! She could just manage, by putting her head down, close to the ground, to *look* through with one eye! But that was *all* she could do. No wonder the poor tall child sat down and cried as if her heart would break.

So she cried, and she cried. And her tears ran down the middle of the hall, like a deep

river.   And very soon there was quite a large
Pool of Tears, reaching half-way down the hall.

And there she might have staid, till this
very day, if the White Rabbit hadn't happened
to come through the hall, on his way to visit
the Duchess.   He was dressed up as grand as
grand could be, and he had a pair of white kid
gloves in one hand, and a little fan in the other
hand: and he kept on muttering to himself "Oh,
the Duchess, the Duchess!   Oh, *won't* she be
savage if I've kept her waiting!"

But he didn't see Alice, you know.   So,
when she began to say "If you please, Sir ——"
her voice seemed to come from the top of the
hall, because her head was so high up.   And the
Rabbit was dreadfully frightened: and he dropped
the gloves and the fan, and ran away as hard as
he could go.

Then a *very* curious thing indeed happened.
Alice took up the fan, and began to fan herself
with it: and, lo and behold, she got quite small
again, and, all in a minute, she was just about
the size of a mouse!

Now look at the picture, and you'll soon guess what happened next. It looks just like the sea, doesn't it? But it *really* is the Pool of Tears —— all made of *Alice's* tears, you know!

And Alice has tumbled into the Pool: and the Mouse has tumbled in: and there they are, swimming about together.

Doesn't Alice look pretty, as she swims across the picture? You can just see her blue stockings, far away under the water.

But why is the Mouse swimming away from Alice in such a hurry? Well, the reason is, that Alice began talking about cats and dogs: and a Mouse always *hates* talking about cats and dogs!

Suppose *you* were swimming about, in a Pool of your own Tears: and suppose somebody began talking to *you* about lesson-books and bottles of medicine, wouldn't *you* swim away as hard as you could go?

IV.

THE CAUCUS-RACE.

WHEN Alice and the Mouse had got out of the Pool of Tears, of course they were very wet: and so were a lot of other curious creatures, that had tumbled in as well. There was a Dodo (that's the great bird, in front, leaning on a walking-stick); and a Duck; and a Lory (that's just behind the Duck, looking over its head); and an Eaglet (that's on the left-hand side of the Lory); and several others.

Well, and so they didn't know how in the world they were to get dry again. But the Dodo —— who was a very wise bird —— told them the right way was to have a Caucus-Race. And what do you think *that* was?

You don't know? Well, you *are* an ignorant child! Now, be very attentive, and I'll soon cure you of your ignorance!

First, you must have a *racecourse*.   It ought to be a *sort* of circle, but it doesn't much matter *what* shape it is, so long as it goes a good way round, and joins on to itself again.

Then, you must put all the *racers* on the course, here and there : it doesn't matter *where*, so long as you don't crowd them too much together.

Then, you needn't say "One, two, three, and away!" but let them all set off running just when they like, and leave off just when they like.

So all these creatures, Alice and all, went on running round and round, till they were all quite dry again.   And then the Dodo said *everybody* had won, and *everybody* must have prizes!

Of course *Alice* had to give them their prizes. And she had nothing to give them but a few comfits she happened to have in her pocket.   And there was just one a - piece, all round.   And there was no prize for Alice!

So what do you think they did?   Alice had nothing left but her thimble.   Now look at the picture, and you'll see what happened.

"Hand it over here!" said the Dodo.

Then the Dodo took the thimble and handed it back to Alice, and said "We beg your acceptance of this elegant thimble!" And then all the other creatures cheered.

Wasn't *that* a curious sort of present to give her?   Suppose they wanted to give *you* a birth-day-present, would you rather they should go to your toy-cupboard, and pick out your nicest doll, and say "Here, my love, here's a lovely birthday-present for you!" or would you like them to give you something *new*, something that *didn't* belong to you before?

V.

BILL, THE LIZARD.

Now I'm going to tell you about Alice's Adventures in the White Rabbit's house.

Do you remember how the Rabbit dropped his gloves and his fan, when he was so frightened at hearing Alice's voice, that seemed to come down from the sky? Well, of course he couldn't go to visit the Duchess *without* his gloves and his fan: so, after a bit, he came back again to look for them.

By this time the Dodo and all the other curious creatures had gone away, and Alice was wandering about all alone.

So what do you think he did? Actually he thought she was his housemaid, and began ordering her about! "Mary Ann!" he said. "Go home this very minute, and fetch me a pair of gloves and a fan! Quick, now!"

Perhaps he couldn't see very clearly with his pink eyes: for I'm sure Alice doesn't look very *like* a housemaid, *does* she? However she was a very good-natured little girl: so she wasn't a bit offended, but ran off to the Rabbit's house as quick as she could.

It was lucky she found the door open: for, if she had had to ring, I suppose the *real* Mary Ann would have come to open the door: and she would *never* have let Alice come in. And I'm sure it was *very* lucky she didn't meet the real Mary Ann, as she trotted upstairs: for I'm afraid she would have taken Alice for a robber!

So at last she found her way into the Rabbit's room: and there was a pair of gloves lying on the table, and she was just going to take them up and go away, when she happened to see a little bottle on the table. And of course it had the words "DRINK ME!" on the label. And of course Alice drank some!

Well, I think that was *rather* lucky, too : don't *you?* For, if she *hadn't* drunk any, all this wonderful adventure, that I'm going to tell you about, wouldn't have happened at all. And wouldn't *that* have been a pity?

You're getting so used to Alice's Adventures, that I daresay you can guess what happened next? If you ca'n't, I'll tell you.

She grew, and she grew, and she grew. And in a very short time the room was full of *Alice :* just in the same way as a jar is full of jam ! There was *Alice* all the way up to the ceiling : and *Alice* in every corner of the room !

The door opened inwards: so of course there wasn't any room to open it: so when the Rabbit got tired of waiting, and came to fetch his gloves for himself, of course he couldn't get in.

So what do you think he did? (Now we come to the picture). He sent Bill, the Lizard, up to the roof of the house, and told him to get down the chimney. But Alice happened to have one of her feet in the fire-place: so, when she heard Bill coming down the chimney, she just gave a little tiny kick, and away went Bill, flying up into the sky!

Poor little Bill! Don't you pity him very much? How frightened he must have been!

VI.

THE DEAR LITTLE PUPPY.

WELL, it doesn't look such a very *little* Puppy, does it? But then, you see, Alice had grown very small indeed : and *that's* what makes the Puppy look so large. When Alice had eaten one of those little magic cakes, that she found in the White Rabbit's house, it made her get quite small, directly, so that she could get through the door : or else she could *never* have got out of the house again. Wouldn't *that* have been a pity? Because then she wouldn't have dreamed all the other curious things that we're going to read about.

So it really *was* a *little* Puppy, you see. And isn't it a little *pet*? And look at the way

it's barking at the little stick that Alice is holding
out for it!   You can see she was a *little* afraid
of it, all the time, because she's got behind that
great thistle, for fear it should run over her.
That would have been just about as bad, for *her*,
as it would be for *you* to be run over by a
waggon and four horses!

   Have you got a little pet puppy at *your*
home?   If you have, I hope you're always kind
to it, and give it nice things to eat.

   Once upon a time, I knew some little
children, about as big as you ; and they had a
little pet dog of their own ; and it was called
Dash.   And this is what they told me about its
birthday - treat.

   " Do you know, one day we remembered it
was Dash's birthday that day.   So we said ' Let's
give Dash a nice birthday-treat, like what we
have on *our* birthdays ! '   So we thought and we
thought ' Now, what is it *we* like best of all,
on *our* birthdays ? '   And we thought and we
thought.   And at last we all called out together
' Why,   its *oatmeal - porridge*, of course ! '   So of

course we thought Dash would be *quite* sure to
like it very much, too.

" So we went to the cook, and we got her to make a saucerful of nice oatmeal - porridge. And then we called Dash into the house, and we said 'Now, Dash, you're going to have your birthday-treat!' We expected Dash would jump for joy : but it didn't, one bit!

" So we put the saucer down before it, and we said 'Now, Dash, don't be greedy! Eat it nicely, like a good dog!'

" So Dash just tasted it with the tip of its tongue : and then it made, oh, such a horrid face! And then, do you know, it did *hate* it so, it wouldn't eat a bit more of it! So we had to put it all down its throat with a spoon!"

I wonder if Alice will give *this* little Puppy some porridge? I don't think she *can*, because she hasn't got any with her. I can't see any saucer in the picture.

VII.

THE BLUE CATERPILLAR.

WOULD you like to know what happened to Alice, after she had got away from the Puppy? It was far too large an animal, you know, for *her* to play with. (I don't suppose *you* would much enjoy playing with a young Hippopotamus, would you? You would always be expecting to be crushed as flat as a pancake under its great heavy feet!) So Alice was very glad to run away, while it wasn't looking.

Well, she wandered up and down, and didn't know what in the world to do, to make herself grow up to her right size again. Of course she knew that she had to eat or drink *something* : that was the regular rule, you know : but she couldn't guess *what* thing.

However, she soon came to a great mushroom, that was so tall that she couldn't see over
the top of it without standing on tip-toe.   And
what do you think she saw?   Something that
I'm sure *you* never talked to, in all your life!

It was a large Blue Caterpillar.

I'll tell you, soon, what Alice and the Caterpillar talked about : but first let us have a good look at the picture.

That curious thing, standing in front of the Caterpillar, is called a " hookah " : and it's used for smoking. The smoke comes through that long tube, that winds round and round like a serpent.

And do you see its long nose and chin? At least, they *look* exactly like a nose and chin, don't they? But they really *are* two of its legs. You know a Caterpillar has got *quantities* of legs : you can see some more of them, further down.

What a bother it must be to a Caterpillar, counting over such a lot of legs, every night, to make sure it hasn't lost any of them !

And *another* great bother must be, having to settle *which* leg it had better move first. I think, if *you* had forty or fifty legs, and if you wanted to go a walk, you'd be such a time in settling which leg to begin with, that you'd never go a walk at all !

And what did Alice and the Caterpillar *talk* about, I wonder?

Well, Alice told it how *very* confusing it was, being first one size and then another.

And the Caterpillar asked her if she liked the size she was, just then.

And Alice said she would like to be just a *little* bit larger —— three inches was such a *wretched* height to be! (Just mark off three inches on the wall, about the length of your middle finger, and you'll see what size she was.)

And the Caterpillar told her one side of the mushroom would make her grow *taller*, and the other side would make her grow *shorter*.

So Alice took two little bits of it with her to nibble, and managed to make herself quite a nice comfortable height, before she went on to visit the Duchess.

VIII.

THE PIG-BABY.

Would you like to hear about Alice's visit to the Duchess? It was a very interesting visit indeed, I can assure you.

Of course she knocked at the door to begin with: but nobody came: so she had to open it for herself.

Now, if you look at the picture, you'll see exactly what Alice saw when she got inside.

The door led right into the kitchen, you see. The Duchess sat in the middle of the room, nursing the Baby. The Baby was howling. The soup was boiling. The Cook was stirring the soup. The Cat —— it was a *Cheshire* Cat —— was grinning, as Cheshire Cats always do. All these things were happening just as Alice went in.

The Duchess has a beautiful cap and gown, hasn't she? But I'm afraid she *hasn't* got a very beautiful *face*.

The Baby —— well, I daresay you've seen *several* nicer babies than *that* : and more good-tempered ones, too. However, take a good look at it, and we'll see if you know it again, next time you meet it!

The Cook —— well, you *may* have seen nicer cooks, once or twice.

But I'm nearly sure you've *never* seen a nicer *Cat!* Now *have* you? And *wouldn't* you like to have a Cat of your own, just like that one, with lovely green eyes, and smiling so sweetly?

The Duchess was very rude to Alice. And no wonder. Why, she even called her own *Baby* "Pig!" And it *wasn't* a Pig, *was* it? And she ordered the Cook to chop off Alice's head: though of course the Cook didn't do it: and at last she threw the Baby at her! So Alice caught the Baby, and took it away with her: and I think that was about the best thing she could do.

So she wandered away, through the wood, carrying the ugly little thing with her. And a great job it was to keep hold of it, it wriggled about so. But at last she found out that the *proper* way was, to keep tight hold of its left foot and its right ear.

But don't *you* try to hold on to a Baby like that, my Child! There are not many babies that *like* being nursed in *that* way!

Well, and so the Baby kept grunting, and grunting. so that Alice had to say to it, quite seriously, "If you're going to turn into a *Pig*, my dear, I'll have nothing more to do with you. Mind now!"

And at last she looked down into its face, and what *do* you think had happened to it? Look at the picture, and see if you can guess.

"Why, *that's* not the Baby that Alice was nursing, is it?"

Ah, I *knew* you wouldn't know it again, though I told you to take a good look at it! Yes, it *is* the Baby. And it's turned into a little *Pig!*

So Alice put it down, and let it trot away into the wood. And she said to herself "It was a *very* ugly Baby: but it makes rather a handsome *Pig,* I think."

Don't you think she was right?

IX.

THE CHESHIRE-CAT.

ALL alone, all alone! Poor Alice! No Baby, not even a *Pig* to keep her company!

So you may be sure she was very glad indeed, when she saw the Cheshire - Cat, perched up in a tree, over her head.

The Cat has a very nice smile, no doubt: but just look what a lot of teeth it's got! Isn't Alice just a *little* shy of it?

Well, yes, a *little*. But then, it couldn't help having teeth, you know: and it *could* have helped smiling, supposing it had been cross. So, on the whole, she was *glad*.

Doesn't Alice look very prim, holding her head so straight up, and with her hands behind her, just as if she were going to say her lessons to the Cat!

And that reminds me. There's a little lesson I want to teach *you*, while we're looking at this picture of Alice and the Cat. Now don't be in a bad temper about it, my dear Child! It's a very *little* lesson indeed!

Do you see that Fox-Glove growing close to the tree? And do you know why it's called a *Fox*-Glove? Perhaps you

think it's got something to do with a Fox?
No indeed! *Foxes* never wear Gloves!

The right word is "*Folk's* - Gloves." Did you
ever hear that Fairies used to be called "the
good *Folk* "?

Now we've finished the lesson, and we'll
wait a minute, till you've got your temper again.

Well? Do you feel quite good-natured again?
No temper-ache? No crossness about the corners
of the mouth? Then we'll go on.

" Cheshire Puss!" said Alice. *(Wasn't* that
a pretty name for a Cat?) "Would you tell me
which way I ought to go from here?"

And so the Cheshire-Cat told her which way
she ought to go, if she wanted to visit the Hatter,
and which way to go, to visit the March Hare.
" They're both mad!" said the Cat.

And then the Cat vanished away, just like
the flame of a candle when it goes out!

So Alice set off, to visit the March Hare.
And as she went along, there was the Cat again!
And she told it she didn't *like* it coming and
going so quickly.

So this time the Cat vanished quite slowly, beginning with the tail, and ending with the grin. Wasn't *that* a curious thing, a Grin without any Cat?   Would you like to see one?

If you turn up the corner of this leaf, you'll have Alice looking at the Grin: and she doesn't look a bit more frightened than when she **was looking** at the Cat, *does* she?

X.

THE MAD TEA-PARTY.

THIS is the Mad Tea-Party. You see Alice had left the Cheshire-Cat, and had gone off to see the March Hare and the Hatter, as the Cheshire-Cat had advised her : and she found them having tea under a great tree, with a Dormouse sitting between them.

There were only those three at the table, but there were quantities of tea-cups set all along it. You ca'n't see all the table, you know, and even in the bit you *can* see there are nine cups, counting the one the March Hare has got in his hand.

That's the March Hare, with the long ears, and straws mixed up with his hair. The straws

showed   he   was   mad —— I   don't   know   why.
Never   twist   up   straws   among   *your*   hair,   for   fear
people   should   think   you're   mad !

There   was   a   nice   green   arm-chair   at   the   end
of   the   table,   that   looked   as   if   it   was   just   meant
for   Alice :   so   she   went   and   sat   down   in   it.

Then   she   had   quite   a   long   talk   with   the
March   Hare   and   the   Hatter.   The   Dormouse
didn't   say   much.   You   see   it   was   fast   asleep
generally,   and   it   only   just   woke   up   for   a
moment,   now   and   then.

As   long   as   it   was   asleep,   it   was   very   useful
to   the   March   Hare   and   the   Hatter,   because   it
had   a   nice   round   soft   head,   just   like   a   pillow :
so   they   could   put   their   elbows   on   it,   and   lean
across   it,   and   talk   to   each   other   quite   comfort-
ably.   You   wouldn't   like   people   to   use   *your*   head
for   a   pillow,   *would*   you ?   But   if   you   were   fast
asleep,   like   the   Dormouse,   you   wouldn't   feel   it :
so   I   suppose   you   wouldn't   care   about   it.

I'm   afraid   they   gave   Alice   *very*   little   to   eat
and   drink.   However,   after   a   bit,   she   helped
herself   to   some   tea   and   bread - and - butter :   only

I don't quite see where she *got* the bread - and - butter : and she had no plate for it. Nobody seems to have a plate except the Hatter. I believe the March Hare must have had one as well : because, when they all moved one place on (that was the rule at this curious tea - party), and Alice had to go into the place of the March Hare, she found he had just up- set the milk - jug into his plate. So I suppose

his plate and the milk - jug are hidden behind
that large tea - pot.

The Hatter used to carry about hats to sell :
and even the one that he's got on his head is
meant to be sold.   You see it's got its price
marked on it ——— a " 10 " and a " 6 " ——— that
means " ten shillings and sixpence."   Wasn't that
a funny way of selling hats ?   And hasn't he got
a beautiful neck - tie on ?   Such a lovely yellow
tie, with large red spots.

He has just got up to say to Alice " Your
hair wants cutting ! "   That was a rude thing to
say, *wasn't* it ?   And do you think her hair *does*
want cutting ?   *I* think it's a very pretty length
——— just the right length.

XI.

THE QUEEN'S GARDEN.

THIS is a little bit of the beautiful garden I told you about. You see Alice had managed at last to get quite small, so that she could go through the little door. I suppose she was about as tall as a mouse, if it stood on its hind-legs: so of course this was a *very* tiny rose-tree: and these are *very* tiny gardeners.

What funny little men they are! But *are* they men, do you think? I think they must be live cards, with just a head, and arms, and legs, so as to *look* like little men. And what *are* they doing with that red paint, I wonder? Well, you see, this is what they told Alice

The Queen of Hearts wanted to have a *red* rose -
tree just in that corner : and these poor little
gardeners had made a great mistake, and had
put in a *white* one instead : and they were so
frightened about it, because the Queen was *sure*
to be angry, and then she would order all their
heads to be cut off !

She was a dreadfully savage Queen, and that was the way she always did, when she was angry with people. " Off with their heads ! " They didn't *really* cut their heads off, you know : because nobody ever obeyed her : but that was what she always *said*.

Now ca'n't you guess what the poor little gardeners are trying to do ? They're trying to paint the roses *red*, and they're in a great hurry to get it done before the Queen comes. And then *perhaps* the Queen won't find out it was a *white* rose - tree to begin with : and then *perhaps* the little men won't get their heads cut off !

You see there were *five* large white roses on the tree —— such a job to get them all painted red ! But they've got three and a half done, now, and if only they wouldn't stop to, talk —— work away, little men, *do* work away ! Or the Queen will be coming before it's done ! And if she finds any *white* roses on the tree, do you know what will happen ? It will be "Off with their heads ! " Oh, work away, my little men ! Hurry, hurry !

The Queen has come!   And *isn't* she angry?
Oh, my poor little Alice!

XII.

THE LOBSTER - QUADRILLE.

Dɪᴅ you ever play at Croquet? There are large wooden balls, painted with different colours, that you have to roll about; and arches of wire, that you have to send them through; and great wooden mallets, with long handles, to knock the balls about with.

Now look at the picture, and you'll see that *Alice* has just been playing a Game of Croquet.

"But she *couldn't* play, with that great red what's - its - name in her arms! Why, how could she hold the mallet?"

Why, my dear Child, that great red what's-its - name (its *real* name is "*a Flamingo*") *is* the mallet! In this Croquet - Game, the balls were

live *Hedge-hogs* —— you know a hedge-hog can roll itself up into a ball? —— and the mallets were live *Flamingos!*

So Alice is just resting from the Game, for a minute, to have a chat with that dear old thing, the Duchess: and of course she keeps her mallet under her arm, so as not to lose it.

"But I don't think she *was* a dear old thing, one bit! To call her Baby a *Pig*, and to want to chop off Alice's head!"

Oh, that was only a joke, about chopping off Alice's head: and as to the Baby —— why, it *was* a Pig, you know! And just look at her *smile!* Why, it's wider than all Alice's head: and yet you can only see half of it!

Well, they'd only had a *very* little chat, when the Queen came and took Alice away, to see the Gryphon and the Mock Turtle.

You don't know what a Gryphon is? Well! Do you know *anything?* That's the question. However, look at the picture. That creature with a red head, and red claws, and green scales, is the *Gryphon*. Now you know.

And the other's the *Mock Turtle*. It's got a calf's - head, because calf's - head is used to make *Mock Turtle Soup*. Now you know.

"But what are they *doing*, going round and round Alice like that?"

Why, I thought of *course* you'd know *that!* They're dancing *a Lobster - Quadrille*.

And next time *you* meet a Gryphon and a
Mock Turtle, I daresay they'll dance it for *you*,
if you ask them prettily.   Only don't let them
come *quite* close, or they'll be treading on your
toes, as they did on poor Alice's.

XIII.

WHO STOLE THE TARTS?

DID you ever hear how the Queen of Hearts made some tarts ? And can you tell me what became of them ?

"Why, of *course* I can ! Doesn't the song tell all about it ?

> *The Queen of Hearts, she made some tarts :*
> *All on a summer day :*
> *The Knave of Hearts, he stole those tarts,*
> *And took them quite away !*"

Well, yes, the *Song* says so. But it would never do to punish the poor Knave, just because there was a *Song* about him. They had to take

him prisoner, and put chains on his wrists, and
bring him before the King of Hearts, so that
there might be a regular trial.

Now, if you look at the big picture, at the
beginning of this book, you'll see what a grand
thing a trial is, when the Judge is a King!

The King is very grand, *isn't* he?   But he
doesn't look very *happy*.   I think that big crown,
on the top of his wig, must be *very* heavy and
uncomfortable.   But he had to wear them *both*,
you see, so that people might know he was a
Judge *and* a King.

And *doesn't* the Queen look cross?   She can
see the dish of tarts on the table, that she had
taken such trouble to make.   And she can see
the bad Knave (do you see the chains hanging
from his wrists?) that stole them away from
her : so I don't think it's any wonder if she *does*
feel a *little* cross.

The White Rabbit is standing near the
King, reading out the Song, to tell everybody
what a bad Knave he is : and the Jury (you
can just see two of them, up in the Jury - box,

the Frog and the Duck) have to settle whether
he's "guilty" or "not guilty."

Now I'll tell you about the accident that
happened to Alice.

You see, she was sitting close by the Jury-
box : and she was called as a witness. You
know what a "witness" is? A "witness" is a
person who has seen the prisoner do whatever
he's accused of, or at any rate knows *something*
that's important in the trial.

But *Alice* hadn't seen the **Queen** *make* the
tarts : and she hadn't seen the **Knave** *take* the
tarts : and, in fact, she didn't know anything
about it : so why in the world they wanted *her*
to be a witness, I'm sure *I* ca'n't tell you!

Anyhow, they *did* want her. And the White
Rabbit blew his big trumpet, and shouted out
"Alice!" And so Alice jumped up in a great
hurry. And then——

And then what *do* you think happened?
Why, her skirt caught against the Jury - box, and
tipped it over, and all the poor little **Jurors** came
tumbling out of it!

Let's try if we can make out all the twelve.
You know there ought to be twelve to make up

a Jury. I see the Frog, and the Dormouse, and the Rat and the Ferret, and the Hedgehog, and the Lizard, and the Bantam - Cock, and the Mole, and the Duck, and the Squirrel, and a screaming bird, with a long beak, just behind the Mole.

But that only makes eleven : we must find one more creature.

Oh, do you see a little white head, coming out behind the Mole, and just under the Duck's beak ? That makes up the twelve.

Mr. Tenniel says the screaming bird is a *Storkling* (of course you know what *that* is ?) and the little white head is a *Mouseling*. Isn't it a little *darling?*

Alice picked them all up again, very carefully, and I hope they weren't *much* hurt !

XIV.

THE SHOWER OF CARDS.

OH dear, oh dear! What *is* it all about? And what's happening to Alice?

Well, I'll tell you all about it, as well I can. The way the trial ended was this. The King wanted the Jury to settle whether the Knave of Hearts was *guilty* or *not guilty* —— that means that they were to settle whether *he* had stolen the Tarts, or if somebody else had taken them. But the wicked *Queen* wanted to have his *punishment* settled, first of all. That wasn't at all fair, *was* it? Because, you know, supposing he never *took* the Tarts, then of course he oughtn't to be punished. Would *you* like to be punished for something you hadn't done?

So Alice said "Stuff and nonsense!"

So the Queen said "Off with her head!" (Just what she always said, when she was angry.)

So Alice said "Who cares for *you?* You're nothing but a pack of cards!"

So they were *all* very angry, and flew up into the air, and came tumbling down again, all over Alice, just like a shower of rain.

And I think you'll *never* guess what happened next. The next thing was, Alice woke up out of her curious dream. And she found that the cards were only some leaves off the tree, that the wind had blown down upon her face.

Wouldn't it be a nice thing to have a curious dream, just like Alice?

The best plan is this. First lie down under a tree, and wait till a White Rabbit runs by, with a watch in his hand: then shut your eyes, and pretend to be dear little Alice.

Good-bye, Alice dear, good-bye!

THE END.

[TURN OVER.

AN EASTER GREETING

TO

EVERY CHILD WHO LOVES "ALICE."

———————————

MY DEAR CHILD,

    Please to fancy, if you can, that you are reading a real letter, from a real friend whom you have seen, and whose voice you can seem to yourself to hear, wishing you, as I do now with all my heart, a happy Easter.

    Do you know that delicious dreamy feeling, when one first wakes on a summer morning, with the twitter of birds in the air, and the fresh breeze coming in at the open window —— when, lying lazily with eyes half shut, one sees as in a dream green boughs waving, or waters rippling in a golden light? It is a pleasure very near to sadness, bringing tears to one's eyes like a beautiful picture or poem. And is not that a Mother's gentle hand that undraws your curtains, and a Mother's sweet voice that summons you to rise? To rise and forget, in the bright sunlight, the ugly dreams that frightened you so when all was dark—— to rise and enjoy another happy day, first kneeling to thank that unseen Friend who sends you the beautiful sun?

Are these strange words from a writer of such tales as "Alice"? And is this a strange letter to find in a book of nonsense? It may be so. Some perhaps may blame me for thus mixing together things grave and gay; others may smile and think it odd that any one should speak of solemn things at all, except in Church and on a Sunday: but I think—— nay, I am sure—— that some children will read this gently and lovingly, and in the spirit in which I have written it.

For I do not believe God means us thus to divide life into two halves—— to wear a grave face on Sunday, and to think it out-of-place to even so much as mention Him on a week-day. Do you think He cares to see only kneeling figures and to hear only tones of prayer—— and that He does not also love to see the lambs leaping in the sunlight, and to hear the merry voices of the children, as they roll among the hay? Surely their innocent laughter is as sweet in His ears as the grandest anthem that ever rolled up from the "dim religious light" of some solemn cathedral?

And if I have written anything to add to those stores of innocent and healthy amusement that are laid up in books for the children I love so well, it is surely something I may hope to look back upon without shame and sorrow (as how much of life must then be recalled!) when my turn comes to walk through the valley of shadows.

This Easter sun will rise on you, dear child, "feeling your life in every limb," and eager to rush out into the fresh morning air——and many an Easter-day will come and go, before it finds you feeble and grey-headed, creeping wearily out to bask once more in the sunlight——but it is good, even now, to think sometimes of that great morning when "the Sun of righteousness" shall "arise with healing in his wings."

Surely your gladness need not be the less for the thought that you will one day see a brighter dawn than this——when lovelier sights will meet your eyes than any waving trees or rippling waters——when angel-hands shall undraw your curtains, and sweeter tones than ever loving Mother breathed shall wake you to a new and glorious day——and when all the sadness, and the sin, that darkened life on this little earth, shall be forgotten like the dreams of a night that is past!

Your affectionate Friend,

LEWIS CARROLL.

CHRISTMAS GREETINGS.

(FROM A FAIRY TO A CHILD.)

LADY dear, if Fairies may
  For a moment lay aside
Cunning tricks and elfish play,
  'Tis at happy Christmas-tide.

We have heard the children say —
  Gentle children, whom we love —
Long ago, on Christmas Day,
  Came a message from above.

Still, as Christmas-tide comes round,
  They remember it again —
Echo still the joyful sound
  "Peace on earth, good-will to men!"

Yet the hearts must childlike be
  Where such heavenly guests abide:
Unto children, in their glee,
  All the year is Christmas-tide!

Thus, forgetting tricks and play
  For a moment, Lady dear,
We would wish you, if we may,
  Merry Christmas, glad New Year!

LEWIS CARROLL.

CAUTIONS TO READERS.

On August 1st, 1881, a story appeared in *Aunt Judy's Magazine* No. 184, entitled "The Land of Idleness, by LEWIS CARROLL." This story was really written by a lady, FRÄULEIN IDA LACKOWITZ. Acting on her behalf, Mr. CARROLL forwarded it to the Editor : and this led to the mistake of naming him as its author.

In October, 1887, the writer of an article on "Literature for the Little ones," in *The Nineteenth Century*, stated that, in 1864, "TOM HOOD was delighting the world with such works as *From Nowhere to the North Pole*. Between TOM HOOD and Mr. LEWIS CARROLL there is more than a suspicion of resemblance in some particulars. *Alice's Adventures in Wonderland* narrowly escapes challenging a comparison with *From Nowhere to the North Pole*. The idea of both is so similar that Mr. CARROLL can hardly have been surprised if some people have believed he was inspired by HOOD." The date 1864 is a mistake. *From Nowhere to the North Pole* was first published in 1874.

*E. Gertrude Thomson's design for the back cover
of the original edition*

ALICE'S ADVENTURES UNDER GROUND

As is generally known, Alice's adventures were "born on a golden afternoon" in July 1862, when the Rev. Charles Lutwidge Dodgson (better known as Lewis Carroll) took the three small daughters of Dean Liddell of Christ Church, Oxford, on a boating trip up the Isis. Carroll delighted the three children by relating Alice's adventures, and eventually promised his favorite among the three, Alice Liddell, to write the story down for her.

At Christmas 1864 Alice Liddell received a remarkable present from Lewis Carroll: a white vellum-bound book, in which the story of "Alice's Adventures under Ground" was carefully printed in Carroll's hand, with many illustrations drawn by Carroll himself, giving his conceptions of the White Rabbit, Alice herself, the Gryphon, the "drink me" episode, the caterpillar on the mushroom, "Father William," the trial of the Knave of Hearts, and other familiar persons and scenes.

This manuscript was the original version of the Alice story (apart from whatever lost earlier notes may once have existed), and it is very different from the book "Alice's Adventures in Wonderland" that we all know. Carroll apparently would not consent to publishing "Alice's Adventures under Ground" until 1886, at which time he supervised a facsimile edition of the Liddell manuscript for publication by Macmillan of London. This edition is now a very rare book. As for the manuscript itself, it has had a noteworthy history. After passing through several hands, it became available for sale in New York in 1948. It was purchased for $50,000, and presented to the British Museum, where it now remains.

This present Dover edition of this unique book is much the closest approximation that has ever been made to Carroll's manuscript. It has been prepared from new photographs made from the manuscript, and the title page and dedication page, which Carroll colored elaborately, have been reproduced in their original colors on the front and rear covers of this book. To make the edition complete, material has been included from Carroll's 1886 book edition, including his introduction and postscript, dedicatory verse, and period advertising. Mr. Martin Gardner, one of the world's foremost authorities on Lewis Carroll and author of "The Annotated Alice," has provided a new introduction.

Complete, unabridged reproduction of the original manuscript, with additional material from the Macmillan 1886 edition. Introduction by Martin Gardner.